BUCK'S TOOTH

Diane Kredensor

aladdin PIX

ALADDIN
NEW YORK LONDON TORONTO SYDNEY NEW DELHI

An imprint of Simon & Schuster Children's Publishing Division
1230 Avenue of the Americas, New York, New York 10020
First Aladdin paper-over-board edition May 2015

For information about special discounts for bulk purchases, please contact
Simon & Schuster Special Sales at 1-866-506-1949 or business@simonandschuster.com.
The Simon & Schuster Speakers Bureau can bring authors to your live event.
For more information or to book an event contact the Simon & Schuster Speakers Bureau
at 1-866-248-3049 or visit our website at www.simonspeakers.com.
Designed by Karina Granda
The illustrations for this book were rendered digitally.
The text of this book was set in Avenir LT Std and Grandma.
Manufactured in China 0215 SCP
2 4 6 8 10 9 7 5 3 1
This book has been cataloged with the Library of Congress.
ISBN 978-1-4814-2382-3
ISBN 978-1-4814-2383-0 (eBook)

For Dana and Tina—my Pearls

—D. K.

CHAPTER ONE

This is Buck. He's a beaver.

Like most beavers, Buck had little ears,
a flat tail, thick brown fur, and
big front teeth.

Or in Buck's case, one big, square, front tooth.

Buck didn't like his tooth.

Not one bit.

It's silly.

That tooth ruined everything!

How Buck talked.

How Buck smiled.

How Buck ate.

It did make brushing his teeth easier, but that was about it.

And now, Buck's big, square tooth was about to ruin the BIGGEST event of the year—

The Beaverton Talent Show.

No one in Beaverton would think of missing it.

Once, Jimmy Nagel blew such a big bubble, he flew up into a tree.

Everyone is still talking about when Charlie Lane wiggled his ears, tail, and nose while juggling four apples.

This year Buck and his friends were finally old enough to enter the show.

Donald turned to Buck.

Buck looked from Donald to Pearl to Marvin. "It's a surprise," he said.

CHAPTER TWO

And it was a surprise.

Even to Buck.

He had no idea what his talent was.

Everything he tried to do ended in disaster.

Stilt walking.

Flute playing.

Whistling.

His tooth always got in the way.
Why did Buck have this silly tooth in the first place?

When Buck's tooth had started to grow, it looked different from everyone else's teeth in his family.

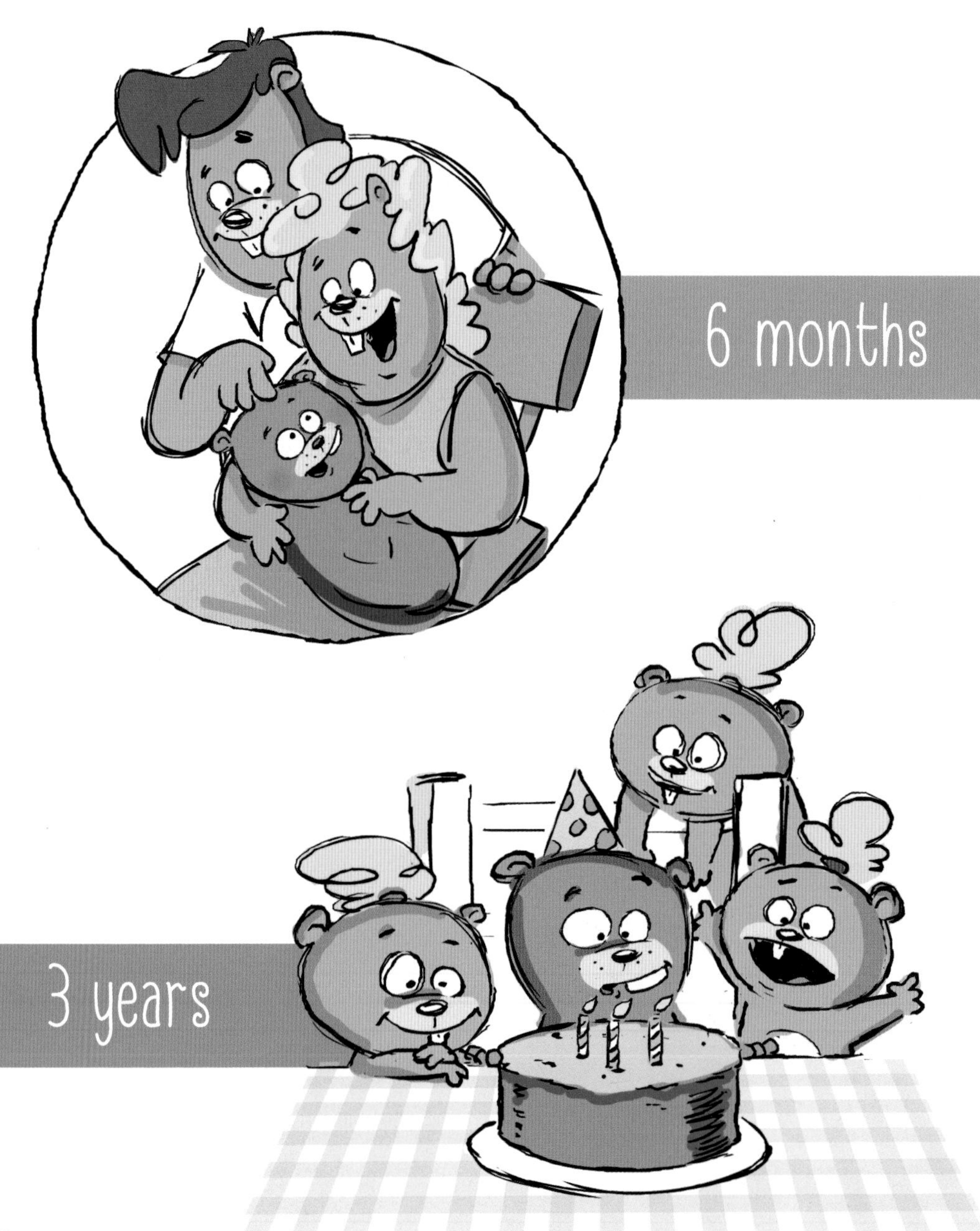

Everyone but . . .

His uncle Henry.

Buck looked exactly like him.

Uncle Henry was a famous sculptor. With his one big tooth he could sculpt just about anyone in Beaverton.

Everyone thought Buck should follow in Uncle Henry's footsteps.

But not Buck.
He didn't want to be in
his uncle's shadow.
Ahhh, my masterpiece
is complete.
BEAVERTON

This is your very first talent show, Bucky.

I remember my first show—I made a toothpick.

What will you be doing?

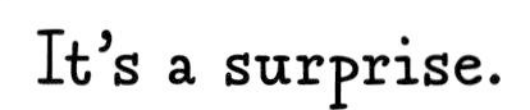

With every step home, Buck grew more worried.

Buck stopped.

For the first time in days, he smiled.

Buck was sure if he got rid of his tooth, he would find his talent.

CHAPTER THREE

Buck hurried home and started planning Operation Tooth Pull.

The next morning, he and his tooth were ready.

Buck started with Plan A. He called his sisters.

Plan A didn't work.

Buck moved on to Plan B.

After opening . . .

thirty pecans,

twenty-two Brazil nuts,

and fifteen walnuts,

Buck's tooth still wouldn't budge.

No problem. There was always Plan C.

Buck went to
Marvin's house.
the GREAT Marvini
The Bunnys
Marvin, I need your help. You're such an awesome magician.
Can you make my tooth disappear?

Buck was sure.

He closed his eyes. He took a deep breath and bid farewell to his tooth.

Buck opened his eyes. His tooth was still there.

Buck's tooth was still there.

No matter what Marvin said, *nothing* happened.

Operation Tooth Pull was officially a failure.

CHAPTER FOUR

Buck wanted to be alone. He went to one of his favorite spots and crawled in.

Buck started to fall asleep when
he heard Pearl calling his name.

Buck didn't answer.

Please?

Please?

P-L-E-E-E-E-E-E-E-A-S-S-S-S-S-S-E!!!!!

Finally, Buck spoke.

At first, Pearl was silent.

But before she left, she told Buck,

Once he was alone again, Buck couldn't stop thinking.

Marvin will make everyone disappear into thin air.
Donald will roll logs down the Mississippi River.
And I'll be left with my tooth.

CHAPER FIVE

While everyone waited for the talent show to begin . . .

Uncle Henry wheeled
his statue to the back of the stage.

Welcome to the twenty-fifth annual Beaverton Talent Show.
There are so many new acts this year.

First up is Holly, Molly, and Polly!

Back at the log, Buck could hear
clapping, laughing, and cheering.
And then he heard singing. It was Pearl!

Uh-oh!

Uh-oh!
BAM!

Uh-oh.
What did I do?
Oh no!
Uncle Henry's masterpiece!

I have to fix it before anyone finds out.

CHAPTER SIX

Frankie McSunders had just finished reciting "Casey at the Bat."

I am so proud to share my latest—and maybe greatest—work in honor of our beloved Beaverton.
Without further ado . . .

Surprise?
BE

The crowd gasped.

BEAVERTON

What are you doing, Buck?
Well, ummm, Molly, I was on my way to the talent show . . .

What have you done?
This looks absolutely . . .

FANTASTIC!
What?
What?
WHAT?

Uncle Henry smiled.

All eyes were on Buck.

Buck realized what he had said.
Then Buck realized what he had done.

BEAVERTON
My tooth!
I used my tooth!

And just like Pearl had said,

Buck's talent was right under his nose the whole time.